Goldwin Smith

Shakespeare, the Man

An attempt to find traces of the dramatist's personal character in his

dramas

Goldwin Smith

Shakespeare, the Man
An attempt to find traces of the dramatist's personal character in his dramas

ISBN/EAN: 9783337394639

Printed in Europe, USA, Canada, Australia, Japan

Cover: Foto ©Andreas Hilbeck / pixelio.de

More available books at **www.hansebooks.com**

SHAKESPEARE:

THE MAN

AN ATTEMPT TO FIND TRACES OF THE
DRAMATIST'S PERSONAL CHARACTER
IN HIS DRAMAS

BY

GOLDWIN SMITH

TORONTO
GEORGE N. MORANG & COMPANY, LIMITED
1899

PREFACE

An attempt to find traces of the personal character of Shakespeare under the dramatist is, it need hardly be said, a different thing from an interpretation of Shakespeare's art. In making it the writer does not trespass on the ground occupied by Coleridge, Gervinus, Dowden, and Hiram Corson.

An apology may seem necessary for quoting in full some well-known passages of Shakespeare ; but the writer does not feel sure that "in these most brisk and giddy-pacéd times," when a tidal-wave of popular and sensational fiction is flowing, familiarity with Shakespeare is so common as it was in former days.

SHAKESPEARE

DRAWN BY MR. JOHN BOADEN FROM THE STRATFORD BUST

Shakespeare: The Man

Such materials as there are for Shakespeare's personal history, or for the history of anyone connected with him, have been gathered with the most loving and persevering industry. Unhappily, they amount to very little. Entries in municipal records, names in a will, a lease, or an inventory, tell hardly anything of the life or character of the man. That orange has now been squeezed dry.

It would seem better worth while to consider under what general influences—social, political, and religious—the life was passed.

7

Shakespeare was a poet of the Renaissance and of the Elizabethan era. Of the Renaissance, with its passion for beauty and art, its joyous release from asceticism, and not only from asceticism, but from strict morality, its tendency to scepticism in religion; of the Elizabethan era with its spring-tide of national life, its heroic struggle against the powers of the past, its love of adventure, its galaxy of active and aspiring spirits in every sphere.

Born in 1564, he would by 1580 be observant and open to impressions. Between 1580 and his death there are thirty-six years full of momentous events; the struggle with Spain; the proclamation of the Papal curse against England in her Queen; the Armada;

8

the conflict in France between the
League and the Huguenots ; the insur-
rection and tragic end of Essex ; the
death of Elizabeth ; the accession of
James ; the union of the Crowns ; the
Gunpowder Plot ; the opening of the
contest between the Stuart King and
his Parliament ; the marriage of the
Princess Elizabeth with the Elector
Palatine ; the beginning of the Thirty
Years' War. During the last two
decades the scene had been changing.
Tudor monarchy and the Renaissance
had been passing away, Puritanism
had developed its force, and the
struggle between a Puritan Parliament and the Crown for supreme
power had begun.

Surroundings must tell, and in the
work even of the most dramatic of

dramatists the man can hardly fail sometimes to appear. There are things which strike us as said for their own sake more than because they fit the particular character; things which seem said with special feeling and emphasis; things which connect themselves naturally with the writer's personal history. There are things which could not be written, even dramatically, by one to whose beliefs and sentiments they were repugnant. Any knowledge which is displayed must of course be the writer's own; so must any proofs of insight, social or of other kinds. Inference as to the writer's character from such passages are precarious, no doubt; yet they may not be altogether futile. Thoroughly dramatic as was the genius of Æschylus and Sophocles, we do not doubt that the character of each, as depicted by Aristophanes in *The Frogs*, is shown. In Corneille and Racine we see little beyond the full-bottomed wig; but in Molière character, sympathies, and antipathies appear.

It must be remembered that Shakespeare had been a poet before he became a playwright.

> *Lorenzo.*—How sweet the moon - light
>   sleeps upon this bank !
> Here will we sit, and let the sounds of
>   musick
> Creep in our ears ; soft stillness, and the
>   night,
> Become the touches of sweet harmony.
> Sit, Jessica : Look how the floor of heaven
> Is thick inlaid with patines of bright gold ;
> There's not the smallest orb, which thou
>   behold'st,
> But in his motion like an angel sings,
> Still quiring to the young-ey'd cherubins :
> Such harmony is in immortal souls ;

11

But, whilst this muddy vesture of decay
Doth grossly close it in, we cannot hear
 it.—
　　　—Merchant of Venice, V., ii.

These lovely lines in *The Merchant of Venice* have no special connection with the characters of Lorenzo and Jessica or with the action. They are a poetic voluntary. Some things in Shakespeare transcends any stage, and would utterly transcend the stage of the Globe theatre. The *Midsummer-Night's Dream* is a supreme creation of aerial fancy, which no gross company of actors and actresses can ever worthily present. In *Hamlet* there is a philosophic poem. All actors fail in the leading part. The man who had the sensibility to feel the part would hardly have stage assurance to act it. The boyish and girlish

12

passion of *Romeo and Juliet,* again, is poetry. No mature actor or actress could feel the passion or present it on the stage.

Ben Jonson says that Shakespeare had " small Latin and less Greek"; Milton says of him that he " warbled his native wood notes wild"; in other words, was not, like Ben Jonson, classically cultured. He had in fact received a common grammar school education, and knew something of Latin and the Latin poets; as in *Love's Labour's Lost* and elsewhere appears.

In Sonnet No. CIV.,

> Three winters' cold
> Have from the forests shook three summers' pride,

is probably a version of Horace's

Sylvis honorem decutit. Shylock's injunction to Jessica recalls the injunction of Horace (*Odes, III.,* 7) to Asterie; and the description of the horse in *Venus and Adonis* is evidently suggested by a passage in the third *Georgic.* Of the "small Latin" there is abundant proof. Of the "less Greek" there is not a trace. Nothing can be less Hellenic than *Troilus and Cressida* or *Timon of Athens.* French, Shakespeare evidently understood. He had read Rabelais, at least he mentions Gargantua. It can hardly be doubted that he understood Italian. But the knowledge which he had practically acquired and carried with him to Town was mainly that of country occupations, of horses and hounds, and of all the flowers

14

upon the bank where the wild thyme grew. To this in Town and afterwards at Court he added a thorough insight into the social world, which shows itself in the well-known advice of Polonius to Laertes, and other passages, such as the advice of Bertram's mother to Bertram in *All's Well that Ends Well*—

> Love all, trust a few,
> Do wrong to none : be able for thine
>   enemy
> Rather in power than use ; and keep thy
>   friend
> Under thy own life's key : be check'd for
>   silence,
> But never tax'd for speech.   —*I., i.*

The advice of Polonius to Laertes may be more certainly set down to the credit of Shakespeare himself, because it really does not well suit the character of Polonius, who is gen-

15

erally represented as a pompous old
fool. A manual of manners and social
conduct might almost be gleaned out
of Shakespeare; and Shakespeare's
social teaching is not like that of
Chesterfield; it has for its basis gen-
uine qualities,—

This above all,—To thine own self be true;
And it must follow as the night the day,
Thou canst not then be false to any man.
—*Hamlet*, I., iii.

That Shakespeare had a cultivated
taste for music, if he was not himself a musician, appears not only from
his anathema upon the man who has
no music in his soul, which would
have borne hard on Dr. Johnson, but
from passages such as the speech of
the Duke in *Twelfth Night* and
that, already mentioned, of Lorenzo
in *The Merchant of Venice*. Fine

music seems to have been Shakespeare's acme of enjoyment.

The attempts to make out that Shakespeare knew law come to nothing. Living in London, he no doubt mingled with Templars as well as with other people, and might easily pick up some phrases. There is no proof of anything more.

It is deemed by the biographers improbable that Shakespeare had travelled. In *Love's Labour's Lost*, Act III., Scene i., the old reading is

> This Signior Julio's giant-dwarf,
> Dan Cupid.

For this has been conjecturally substituted by critics who did not understand the allusion,

> This senior-junior, giant-dwarf,
> Dan Cupid,

which is nonsense.

17

Julio Romano, in a fresco in the Vatican, introduced the figure of Gradasso, "a giant-dwarf" of pigmy stature but great muscular power, thus resembling Cupid in the combination of diminutiveness and might. To this fresco Shakespeare evidently refers. Had he seen it? In the *Winter's Tale*, Act V., Scene ii., he expresses his admiration of Romano, though, curiously enough, not as a painter but as a sculptor—

Third Gentleman.—No : the princess hearing of her mother's statue, which is in the keeping of Paulina,—a piece many years in doing, and now newly performed by that rare Italian master, Julio Romano; who, had he himself eternity, and could put breath into his work, would beguile nature of her custom, so perfectly he is her ape.

Shakespeare's pictures of Italian life seem to show familiarity with it, and his epithets, such as "old Verona," are apposite. Looseness about Italian geography, if it can be proved, would not be a strong argument on the other side. If an Englishman had travelled anywhere in those days, it would probably have been in Italy.

In history Shakespeare was not learned. He makes the Duke of Austria responsible for the death of Richard I. He follows the chroniclers blindly. On the other hand, he had a wonderful eye for historical character. He dresses his Romans in cloaks and hats; but his delineation of Cæsar, Brutus, Cassius, and Marc Antony cannot be surpassed. "Speak; Cæsar is turned to hear"; and "I rather tell thee what is to

19

be feared, Than what I fear; for always I am Cæsar."

He sometimes betrays what seems strange ignorance. He introduces artillery in the reign of John; gives Bohemia a sea-coast; and introduces nunneries at Athens. But may not this rather be said to be simple disregard of the limitations of time and place? Athens in the *Midsummer-Night's Dream* is not the classic city, but an Italian Duchy of which Theseus is the Duke. When the fashion was introduced of a spectacular representation of Shakespeare's plays and the manager aimed at being strictly historical, some of the results were grotesque. In the *Midsummer-Night's Dream* Lysander and Demetrius were represented as going to fight a duel, a thing wholly foreign to Hellenic ideas, with their Hellenic swords; and Theseus, in classic attire, threatened to put Hermia, also in classic attire, into a nunnery. In *Macbeth*, Shakespeare's idea of the Scotch monarchy no doubt was something magnificently royal, such as might tempt ambition. But the spectacular manager thought he was showing his fidelity to history by introducing the barbarous simplicity of primeval Scotland, and Macbeth was represented as climbing through regicide and crime to the dazzling elevation of a king enthroned on a wooden stool and banqueting on apples.

The mystery of Shakespeare's Sonnets will never be solved. What is

21

certain is that the series is a product
of the Renaissance, sometimes burning
with intense and irregular passion.
Morals of the Court of Elizabeth
were loose, like those of other Courts
of Europe at the time, the vestal vir-
ginity of the Queen notwithstanding.
It seems to be proved that the poet's
marriage with Anne Hathaway took
place not before it was necessary ;
that it was enforced, and that he
afterwards saw little of his wife
and children for eleven years, so
that he might write with feeling,

> War is no strife
> To the dark house and the detested wife.
> —*All's Well that Ends Well, II., iii.*

Prospero's injunction to Ferdinand
in *The Tempest* is so strange and
apparently gratuitous, that we can

hardly help regarding it as an outpouring of the poet's bitter experience.—

> *Prospero.*—Then, as my gift, and thine
>   own acquisition
> Worthily purchased, take my daughter :
>   But
> If thou dost break her virgin knot before
> All sanctimonious ceremonies may
> With full and holy rite be minister'd,
> No sweet aspersion shall the heavens let
>   fall
> To make this contract grow ; but barren
>   hate,
> Sour-ey'd disdain, and discord, shall bestrew
> The union of your bed with weeds so
>   loathly,
> That you shall hate it both : therefore,
>   take heed,
> As Hymen's lamps shall light you.
>   —*The Tempest, IV., i.*

All this considered, we have reason to be thankful for the essential soundness of Shakespeare's morality, especially with regard to marriage. There is not in him anything of the evil spirit of the Restoration drama. Matrimony with him is always holy, and though attacks upon its sanctity form the subject of more than one of his plots, he carries it through them inviolate. There is no Don Juan among his heroes.

It must be owned that in *Measure for Measure*, in some of the Falstaff scenes, and elsewhere, Shakespeare plays with certain subjects in a way suggestive of looseness in sexual morality. There is a curious passage in *Hamlet* (*II., i.*), where Polonius seems to think " drabbing " would not disgrace his son, but that incontinence, by which appears to be meant illicit intercourse with other than courtesans, would. Opinion on these

24

points has greatly advanced since Shakespeare, though governments still bow to supposed necessity.

Too often the poet stoops to obscenities. This is partly the vice of the Renaissance, which shows itself to an extreme extent in Rabelais. Partly, it is the mark of the ages before delicacy, which gave birth to Boccaccio. Partly, perhaps principally, it is a condescension to the tastes of the audience of the Globe Theatre. From Hamlet's advice to the Players, we see that there was a great demand for buffoonery. Perhaps it would be charitable to surmise that Shakespeare sought to embrace the whole of human nature as it presented itself in his time. His obscenity is mere grossness; it is not provocative of lust. At worst, in him all is nature. He is never procurer to the lords of Hell. There is nothing in him so disgusting as the laborious filth offered by Massinger as a tribute to the taste of a vulgar audience in the comic scenes of *The Virgin Martyr.*

Shakespeare is said to have died of the effects of a drinking bout. But if the tradition is true the drinking bout was probably an exception, for he evidently abhors excess.

> *Horatio.* Is it a custom?
> *Hamlet.* Ay, marry, is't :
> But to my mind,—though I am native here,
> And to the manner born,—it is a custom
> More honour'd in the breach, than the
>   observance.
> This heavy-headed revel, east and west,
> Makes us traduc'd, and tax'd of other
>   nations :
> They clepe us, drunkards, and with swin-
>   ish phrase

Soil our addition ; and, indeed, it takes
From our achievements, though perform'd
    at height,
The pith and marrow of our attribute.

          —*Hamlet, I., iv.*

He refers to the same national disgrace in *Othello*, Act II., Scene iii. In the same scene we have—

Cassio.—Not to-night, good Iago ; I have very poor and unhappy brains for drinking : I could well wish courtesy would invent some other custom of entertainment.

Cassio.—O thou invisible spirit of wine, if thou hast no name to be known by, let us call thee—devil !

Cassio.—I remember a mass of things, but nothing distinctly ; a quarrel, but nothing wherefore.—O, that men should put an enemy in their mouths, to steal away their brains ! that we should, with joy, revel, pleasure, and applause, transform ourselves into beasts !

" I will do anything, Nerissa," says Portia, " ere I will be married to a sponge."

> Let me be your servant;
> Though I look old, yet I am strong and
>   lusty;
> For in my youth I never did apply
> Hot and rebellious liquors in my blood:
> Nor did not with unbashful forehead woo
> The means of weakness and debility;
> Therefore my age is as a lusty winter,
> Frosty, but kindly.
>
>   —*As You Like It, II., iii.*

What were Shakespeare's political sentiments? In his time, during the early part of it at least, everybody was royalist. Domestic dissensions were suspended by the struggle with Catholic powers, and the Queen was idolized as impersonating the national cause. Supremely royalist, of course, were the Lord Chamberlain's or the King's Players. In three plays probably, in the *Midsummer-Night's Dream*, in *Henry VIII.*, assuming the genuineness of the passage, and

28

in *The Tempest*, the courtier is distinctly seen.

The *Midsummer-Night's Dream* was apparently performed at some Court marriage, at what marriage we cannot now tell, though the author of the excellent article on Shakespeare in the *Dictionary of National Biography* conjectures that it was either that of Lucy Harrington to Edward Russell, third Earl of Bedford, on the 12th of December, 1594, or that of William Stanley, Earl of Derby, at Greenwich, on the 24th of January, 1594-5. There cannot be a doubt that Elizabeth was present and heard the well-known compliment to the "fair vestal thronéd by the West." But she also heard:

" Thrice blessed they, that master so their
    blood

To undergo such maiden pilgrimage.
But earthlier happy is the rose distilled
Than that, which, withering on the virgin
thorn,
Grows, lives and dies, in single blessed-
ness.''
—*Midsummer-Night's Dream, I., i.*

Was not this advice, most delicately given, to the fair vestal to marry, and thus fulfil the desire of all loyal and Protestant England ?

The Tempest was acted before the Court when Frederick, Elector Palatine, afterwards the luckless King of Bohemia, came over to claim his bride, the Princess Elizabeth, darling of all Protestant hearts. It embodies a Masque, such as was fashionable at weddings, and which was perhaps performed, not by the Players, but by lords and ladies of the Court. There cannot be a doubt that these lines refer to England :—

Iris.—Ceres, most bounteous lady, thy
rich leas
Of wheat, rye, barley, vetches, oats, and
peas ;
Thy turfy mountains, where live nibbling
sheep,
And flat meads, thatch'd with stover, them
to keep ;
Thy banks with peonied and lilied brims,
Which spongy April at thy hest betrims,
To make cold nymphs chaste crowns : and
thy broom groves,
Whose shadow the dismissed bachelor loves,
Being lass-lorn ; thy pole-clipt vineyard ;
And thy sea-marge, steril, and rocky-hard,
Where thou thyself dost air :

—Tempest, IV., i.

The turfy mountains with the nibbling sheep are evidently the downs; and the pole-clipt vineyards are most likely the hop-grounds.

The words of Ferdinand,

Let me live here ever ;
So rare a wonder'd father, and a wife,
Make this place Paradise—

—Tempest, IV., i.

31

would be very apt in the mouth of
the young Elector who had come over
to England to be married to James'
daughter.

It would have been strange if the
learned King James had not taken
to himself the character of Prospero,
" reputed in dignity, and for the
liberal arts without a parallel;" or
if he had not seen in the conspira-
tors of different grades the authors
of the Gunpowder Plot and the
enemies of prerogative in the House
of Commons. He could not have
failed to enjoy such satire on
political agitation as—

Gonzalo.—I' the commonwealth I would
    by contraries
Execute all things : for no kind of traffic
Would I admit ; no name of magistrate ;
Letters should not be known ; riches,
    poverty,

And use of service, none ; contract, suc-
cessions,
Bourn, bound of land, tilth, vineyard, none :
No use of metal, corn, or wine, or oil :
No occupation ; all men idle, all ;
And women too ; but innocent and pure :
No sovereignty :—

> Sebastian.—And yet he would be king
> on't.

> Antonio.—The latter end of his common-
> wealth forgets the beginning.

> Gonzalo.—All things in common, nature
> should produce
Without sweat or endeavour : treason,
felony,
Sword, pike, knife, gun, nor need of any
engine,
Would I not have ; but nature should
bring forth,
Of its own kind, all foizon, all abundance,
To feed my innocent people.

> *—Tempest, II., i.*

Raleigh, who was a courtier, even
to a painful extent, in his *Prerogative of Parliaments* sums up a highly
royalist history of the origin of the
Great Charter by saying that it " had

first an obscure birth from usurpation, and was secondly fostered and showed to the world by rebellion." Shakespeare, in *King John*, says not a word about the Great Charter, or anything connected with it. If the Barons quarrel with the King, it is not about political rights, but on account of the deposition and murder of Arthur. Even that crime is softened by reducing it to intention, Arthur's death being represented as an accident. The submission to the Pope is managed in a way as little humiliating as possible. In the end, John is the national King, supported by English patriots against the French pretender and invader.

Of *Henry VIII.*, though by no means the whole play is Shakespearian, it is pretty certain that the whole passed under Shakespeare's hand, and in it Henry is presented as an august, magnificent and apparently beneficent lord, without a suggestion of the tyrant.

We see, too, where the *Merry Wives of Windsor* was performed,

Mistress Quickly.—About, about ;
Search Windsor castle, elves, within and
    out :
Strew good luck, ouphes, on every sacred
    room ;
That it may stand till the perpetual doom,
In state as wholesome, as in state 'tis fit;
Worthy the owner, and the owner it.
The several chairs of order look you scour
With juice of balm, and every precious
    flower :
Each fair instalment, coat, and several
    crest,
With loyal blazon, evermore be blest !
And nightly, meadow-fairies, look, you
    sing,
Like to the Garter's compass, in a ring :
The expressure that it bears, green let it
    be,

More fertile-fresh than all the field to see ;
And, *Hony soit qui mal y pense*, write,
In emerald tufts, flowers purple, blue and
    white :
Like sapphire, pearl, and rich embroi-
    dery,
Buckled below fair knighthood's bending
    knee :
Fairies use flowers for their charactery.
    —*Merry Wives of Windsor, V., v.*

The strong language about the
divine character of royalty, and the
indelibility of the coronation balm,
put into the mouth of Richard II.,
is in character and may be regarded
as dramatic. On the other hand,
there are pretty strong expressions
about the sacredness of royalty
elsewhere.

               To do this deed,
Promotion follows : If I could find ex-
    ample
Of thousands, that had struck anointed
    Kings,
And flourished after, I'd not do't it : but
    since

Nor brass, nor stone, nor parchment,
bears not one,
Let villainy itself forswear't.

—*Winter's Tale, I., ii.*

And in *Macbeth*, Act II., Scene iii.

MacDuff.—Confusion now hath made
his masterpiece ;
Most sacrilegious murder hath broke ope
The Lord's anointed temple, and stole
thence
The life o' the building.

In *Macbeth*, Act IV., Scene iii., there
is a passage which, if the poet is
speaking, intimates his belief in touch-
ing for the King's Evil.—

Doctor.—Ay, sir : there are a crew of
wretched souls,
That stay his cure : their malady convinces
The great array of art ; but, at his touch,
Such sanctity hath heaven given his hand,
They presently amend.

On the other hand, a popular monarchy, such as James I.'s was not, but

that of his son Henry might have been, is evidently Shakespeare's ideal. He shows it in the dialogue between Henry V. and the soldiers before the battle of Agincourt. His King, however exalted, is a man and not a fetich. " Though I speak it to you," Henry is made to say—

" I think, the king is but a man, as I am ; the violet smells to him, as it doth to me ; the element shows to him, as it doth to me ; all his senses have but human conditions ; his ceremonies laid by, in his nakedness he appears but a man ; and though his affections are higher mounted than ours, yet, when they stoop, they stoop with the like wing ; therefore when he sees reason of fears, as we do, his fears, out of doubt, be of the same relish as ours are : Yet, in reason, no man should possess him with any appearance of fear, lest he, by showing it, should dishearten his army."

—*Henry V., IV., i.*

The dramatist understands that it was by a noble comradeship between

King and soldier and the King's hold
upon the soldier's heart that at Agincourt despair was turned into victory.

The poor condemned English,
Like sacrifices, by their watchful fires
Sit patiently, and inly ruminate
The morning's danger; and their gesture
sad,
Investing lank-lean cheeks, and war-worn
coats,
Presenteth them unto the gazing moon
So many horrid ghosts. O, now, who will
behold
The royal captain of this ruin'd band,
Walking from watch to watch, from tent
to tent,
Let him cry—Praise and glory on his
head !
For forth he goes, and visits all his host;
Bids them good-morrow, with a modest
smile;
And calls them—brothers, friends, and
countrymen.
Upon his royal face there is no note
How dread an army hath enrounded him;
Nor doth he dedicate one jot of colour
Unto the weary and all-watched night;
But freshly looks, and overbears attaint,
With cheerful semblance, and sweet
majesty;

39

That every wretch, pining and pale be-
fore,
Beholding him, plucks comfort from his
looks :
A largess universal, like the sun,
His liberal eye doth give to every one,
Thawing cold fear.
                              —*Henry V., IV.*

The worthlessness of mere state is
one of his commonplaces.

O ceremony, show me but thy worth !
What is the soul of adoration ?
Art thou aught else but place, degree,
and form,
Creating awe and fear in other men ?
Wherein thou art less happy being fear'd,
Than they in fearing.
                              —*Henry V., IV. i.*

Shakespeare in his political and
social sentiment must have been
conservative. We can scarcely doubt
that it is he who speaks in *Troilus
and Cressida* (I., iii.)—

The specialty of rule hath been neglected :
And, look, how many Grecian tents do
stand

Hollow upon this plain, so many hollow
    factions.   .
When that the general is not like the
    hive,
To whom the foragers shall all repair,
What honey is expected ?   Degree being
    vizarded,
The unworthiest shows as fairly in the
    mask.
The heavens themselves, the planets, and
    this center,
Observe degree, priority, and place,
Insisture, course, proportion, season, form,
Office, and custom, in all line of order :
And therefore is the glorious planet, Sol,
In noble eminence enthron'd and spher'd
Amidst the other ;   whose med'cinable
    eye
Corrects the ill aspects of planets evil,
And posts, like the commandment of a
    king,
Sans check, to good and bad : But, when
    the planets,
In evil mixture, to disorder wander,
What plagues, and what portents ? what
    mutiny ?
What ragings of the sea ? shaking of
    earth ?
Commotion in the winds ? frights, changes
    horrors,
Divert and crack, rend and deracinate
The unity and married calm of states

Quite from their fixture ? O, when degree
    is shak'd,
Which is the ladder of all high designs,
The enterprize is sick ! How could com-
    munities,
Degrees in schools, and brotherhoods in citise,
Peaceful commerce from dividable shores,
The primogenitive and due of birth,
Prerogative of age, crowns, sceptres,
    laurels,
But by degree, stand in authentick place ?
Take but degree away, untune that string,
And, hark, what discord follows ! each
    thing meets
In mere oppugnancy : The bounded waters
Should lift their bosoms higher than the
    shores,
And make a sop of all this solid globe :
Strength should be lord of imbecility,
And the rude son should strike his father
    dead :
Force should be right ; or, rather, right
    and wrong,
(Between whose endless jar justice resides,)
Should lose their names, and so should
    justice too.
Then every thing includes itself in power,
Power into will, will into appetite ;
And appetite, an universal wolf,
So doubly seconded with will and power,
Must make perforce an universal prey,
And, last, eat up himself.

42

The following passage, also against democracy, is in the mouth of Coriolanus dramatic, but it is also emphatic,—

> No, take more :
> What may be sworn by, both divine and
>   human,
> Seal what I end withal !—This double
>   worship,—
> Where one part does disdain with cause,
>   the other
> Insult without all reason ; where gentry,
>   title, wisdom
> Cannot conclude, but by the yea and no
> Of general ignorance,—it must omit
> Real necessities, and give way the while
> To unstable slightness ; purposes so barr'd,
>   it follows,
> Nothing is done to purpose : Therefore,
>   beseech you,—
> You that will be less fearful than discreet
> That love the fundamental part of state,
> More than you doubt the change of't ; that
>   prefer
> A noble life before a long, and wish
> To jump a body with a dangerous physick
> That's sure of death without it,—at once
>   pluck out
> The multitudinous tongue, let them not
>   lick

The sweet which is their poison : your dis-
honour
Mangles true judgment, and bereaves the
state
Of that integrity which should become it ;
Not having the power to do the good it
would,
For the ill which doth control it.

—*Coriolanus, III., i.*

It should be remembered that revo-
lution in its most terrible form, that
of the risings of the Anabaptists on
the continent, had not been very long
laid in its grave.

Some passages are instinct with
intense dislike of mobs and mob-
rule. The words in *Coriolanus* are
in character, but they are strong,—

I heard him swear,
Were he to stand for consul, never would
he
Appear i' the market-place, nor on him
put
The napless vesture of humility ;

Nor, showing (as the manner is) his wounds
To the people, beg their stinking breaths.
        —*Coriolanus, II., i.*

So in *Julius Cæsar*, what follows
is full of contempt for the folly
and fickleness of the rabble.—

Casca.—I can as well be hanged, as tell
the manner of it : it was mere foolery. I
did not mark it.   I saw Mark Antony
offer him a crown ;—yet 'twas not a crown
neither, twas one of these coronets ;—and,
as I told you, he put it by once ; but, for
all that, to my thinking, he would fain
have had it.   Then he offered it to him
again ; then he put it by again : but, to
my thinking, he was very loath to lay
his fingers off it.   And then he offered it
the third time ; he put it the third time
by : and still as he refused it, the rab-
blement hooted, and clapped their chopped
hands, and threw up their sweaty night-
caps, and uttered such a deal of stinking
breath because Cæsar refused the crown,
that it had almost choaked Cæsar ; for
he swooned, and fell down at it : And for
mine own part, I durst not laugh, for fear
of opening my lips, and receiving the bad
air.   —*Julius Cæsar, I., ii.*

45

"Stinking breaths," "chopped hands" and "sweaty night caps" are terms not only of aversion but of disgust.

The travesty of Cade's manifesto in *Henry VI.* is fresh at the present day and used as ammunition by modern conservative writers and speakers.

Cade.—Be brave then ; for your captain is brave, and vows reformation. There shall be, in England, seven half-penny loaves sold for a penny ; the three-hooped pot shall have ten hoops ; and I will make it felony, to drink small beer ; all the realm shall be in common, and in Cheapside shall my palfrey go to grass. And, when I am king, (as king I will be)————

All.—God save your majesty !

Cade.—I thank you, good people !—there shall be no money ; all shall eat and drink on my score ; and I will apparel them all in one livery, that they may agree like brothers, and worship me their lord.

—*King Henry VI., Part II., IV., ii.*

Demagogism is an object of dislike.

46

" I love the people," says the Duke
in *Measure for Measure,*

But do not like to stage me to their eyes :
Though it do well, I do not relish well
Their loud applause, and *aves* vehement ;
Nor do I think the man of safe discretion,
That does affect it.

—Measure for Measure, I., i.

At the same time there are not
wanting passages breathing a strong
sense of the injustice and inequali-
ties of society, such as a social
radical might be glad to repeat.

A man may see how this world goes,
with no eyes. Look with thine eyes : see
how yon' justice rails upon yon' simple
thief. Hark, in thine ear : change places ;
and, handy-dandy, which is the justice,
which is the thief ?

—King Lear, IV., vi.

Poor naked wretches, whereso'er you are,
That bide the pelting of this pitiless storm,
How shall your houseless heads, and unfed
    sides,

47

Your loop'd and window'd raggedness de-
 fend you
From seasons such as these? O, I have
 ta'en
Too little care of this! Take physick,
 pomp ;
Expose thyself to feel what wretches feel ;
That thou may'st shake the superflux to
 them,
And show the heavens more just.

—King Lear, III., iv.

Gloster.—Here, take this purse, thou
 whom the heaven's plagues
Have humbled to all strokes : that I am
 wretched,
Makes thee the happier :—Heavens, deal
 so still !
Let the superfluous, and lust-dieted man,
That slaves your ordinance, that will not
 see
Because he doth not feel, feel your power
 quickly ;
So distribution should undo excess,
And each man have enough.

—King Lear, IV., i.

O, that estates, degrees and offices,
Were not deriv'd corruptly ! and that
 clear honour
Were purchas'd by the merit of the
 wearer !

48

How many then should cover, that stand
    bare ?
How many be commanded, .that com-
    mand ?
How much low peasantry would then be
    glean'd
From the true seed of honour ? and how
    much honour
Pick'd from the chaff and ruin of the
    times
To be new varnish'd ?

        —*Merchant of Venice, II., ix.*

In a passage in *Romeo and Juliet*
there is a touch of sympathy for
the castaway.

Art thou so bare, and full of wretchedness,
And fear'st to die ? famine is in thy cheeks,
Need and oppression starveth in thy eyes,
Upon thy back hangs ragged misery,
The world is not thy friend, nor the
    world's law :
The world affords no law to make thee
    rich ;
Then be not poor, but break it, and take
    this.
        —*Romeo and Juliet, V., i.*

With all his feeling for the glory

of Henry V., Shakespeare shows his
sense of the waste of lives in iniqui-
tous wars.—

> *Captain.*—Truly to speak, sir, and with
>   no addition,
> We go to gain a little patch of ground,
> That hath in it no profit but the name.
> To pay five ducats, five, I would not farm
>   it ;
> Nor will it yield to Norway, or the Pole,
> A ranker rate, should it be sold in fee.
>   *Hamlet.*—Why, then the Polack never
>   will defend it.
>   *Captain.*—Yes, 'tis already garrisoned.
>   *Hamlet.* — Two thousand souls, and
>   twenty thousand ducats,
> Will not debate the question of this
>   straw :
> This is the imposthume of much wealth
>   and peace ;
> That inward breaks, and shows no cause
>   without
> Why the man dies.
>
> — *Hamlet, IV., iv.*

There are passages expressive of a
sympathy for the sufferings of animals
which appears to be heart-felt.

Duke Senior.—Come, shall we go and kill us venison?
And yet it irks me, the poor dappled fools,—
Being native burghers of this desert city,—
Should, in their own confines, with forked heads
Have their round haunches gor'd.
  First Lord.—   Indeed, my lord,
The melancholy Jaques grieves at that ;
And, in that kind, swears you do more usurp
Than doth your brother that hath banish'd you.
To-day, my lord of Amiens, and myself,
Did steal behind him, as he lay along
Under an oak, whose antique root peeps out
Upon the brook that brawls along this wood :
To the which place a poor sequester'd stag,
That from the hunters' aim had ta'en a hurt,
Did come to languish ; and, indeed, my lord,
The wretched animal heav'd forth such groans,
That their discharge did stretch his leathern coat
Almost to bursting ; and the big round tears

Cours'd one another down his innocent
    nose
In piteous chase ; and thus the hairy fool,
Much marked of the melancholy Jaques,
Stood on the extremest verge of the swift
    brook,
Augmenting it with tears.

—As You Like It, II., i.

So the Princess in *Love's Labour's Lost*, Act IV., Scene i.,—

As I, for praise alone, now seek to spill
The poor deer's blood, that my heart
    means no ill.

Of the passage in the second part of *Henry VI.*, (III., i.), pathetically describing the calf driven to the slaughter house of the butcher, and the dam wailing for her young one, perhaps no more can safely be said than that it passed under the hand of Shakespeare.

The language which passes between

men and women in the plays is sometimes indelicate and such as at the
present day would imply a low estimate of womanhood. But this is of
the time. Queen Elizabeth was no
paragon of delicacy either in manners
or in language. That Shakespeare's
estimate of womanhood was not low
he has shown by giving us a gal-
lery of female characters ranging in
variety, within female limits, from
Beatrice to Juliet or Hero; but all
supreme in beauty and loveliness.
There are bad women of course, such as
Regan, Goneril, and Lady Macbeth,
though in Lady Macbeth, with all
her wickedness and masculine daring, there is nothing unqueenly.
Brothel-keepers and abandoned women are a class apart, too familiar

to Shakespeare, but not more familiar to him than to other writers and to people generally in that age. We appreciate Shakespeare's treatment of the female character more highly when we consider how unfavourable in all probability his experience had been.

Shakespeare lived long before the advent of the New Woman, and in a state of society when the weaker vessel was more dependent for protection on the stronger than it is now. But it would be difficult, whatever the state of society might be, to reconcile Shakespeare's view of the relation between husband and wife with that of John Stuart Mill or his female disciples. *The Taming of the Shrew* is broad farce, though perhaps not without a more serious undertone; and we may set down as dramatic the ultra-conjugal speech of the Shrew at the end of the play which she ends by putting her hand under her husband's foot; though there are some points in it which might deserve the attention of ladies who declaim against the tyranny of man, as if he had done nothing for woman. There is nothing farcical, however, in the words of Beatrice in *Much Ado About Nothing*,—

> And, Benedick, love on, I will requite
>   thee ;
> Taming my wild heart to thy loving
>   hand.
>   *—III., i.*

Or in those of Portia in *The Merchant of Venice*,—

Portia.—You see me, lord Bassanio,
   where I stand,
Such as I am : though, for myself alone,
I would not be ambitious in my wish.
To wish myself much better ; yet, for
   you,
I would be trebled twenty times myself;
A thousand times more fair, ten thousand
   times
More rich ;
That only to stand high on your account,
I might in virtues, beauties, livings,
   friends,
Exceed account : but the full sum of me
Is sum of something : which, to term in
   gross,
Is an unlesson'd girl, unschool'd, un-
   practis'd :
Happy in this, she is not yet so old
But she may learn : and happier than
   this,
She is not bred so dull but she can
   learn ;
Happiest of all, is, that her gentle spirit
Commits itself to yours to be directed,
As from her lord, her governor, her king.
Myself, and what is mine, to you, and
   yours
Is now converted : but now I was the lord
Of this fair mansion, master of my ser-
   vants,
Queen o'er myself ; and even now, but now,

This house, these servants, and this same
    myself,
Are yours, my lord ; I give them with
    this ring ;
Which when you part from, lose, or give
    away,
Let it presage the ruin of your love,
And be my vantage to exclaim on you.

—*III.*, *ii.*

The sanctity of the marriage tie, as
was said before, is presented with
the poet's full power.

Portia's success as an advocate
cannot be pleaded as encouraging to
ladies to enter the legal profession.
It will be observed that she gets not
only her garments but her notes
from her cousin Doctor Bellario at
Padua.

There is in *Love's Labour's Lost* a
passage highly complimentary to the
female intellect.

57

For when would you, my lord, or you,
   or you,
Have found the ground of study's excel-
   lence,
Without the beauty of a woman's face?
From women's eyes this doctrine I derive:
They are the ground, the books, the acade-
   mes,
From whence doth spring the true Pro-
   methean fire.
Why, universal plodding prisons up
The nimble spirits in the arteries;
As motion, and long-during action, tires
The sinewy vigour of the traveller.
Now, for not looking on a woman's face,
You have in that forsworn the use of
   eyes;
And study, too, the causer of your vow:
For where is any author in the world,
Teaches such beauty as a woman's eye?

                  —IV., iii.

Shakespeare's moral philosophy is sound, but tolerant and liberal. He seems to have suspected that the bounds between virtue and vice were less clear, and that characters were more mixed than moralists commonly assumed. He sees "a soul of goodness in things evil." " The web of our life," he says, "is of a mingled yarn, good and ill together : our virtues would be proud, if our faults whipp'd them not ; and our crimes would despair, if they were not cherished by our virtues" (*All's Well that Ends Well, IV., iii.*)

It has been remarked that there is not the slightest allusion to the grand struggle with Spain or to the Armada. The account of this may be that Shakespeare was a Court playwright, and that war with Spain was not, of all subjects, the most palatable to the Court. War with Spain was forced on Elizabeth ; but her own leanings probably were rather Spanish ; so, even more decidedly were those of her successor. Spain was the Grand Monarchy, and the alliance had natural attractions for Princes, especially if their subjects were supposed to be mutinous. Shakespeare, however, like a true dramatist, was unpolitical.

It was not from want of patriotism, at all events, that he makes no reference to the war with Spain and the Armada. English feeling in him is very strong.

This royal throne of kings, this scepter'd
    isle,
This earth of majesty, this seat of Mars,
This other Eden, demi-paradise ;
This fortress, built by nature for herself,
Against infection, and the hand of war :
This happy breed of men, this little
    world ;
This precious stone set in the silver sea,
Which serves it in the office of a wall,

Or as a moat defensive to a house,
Against the envy of less happier lands ;
This blessed plot, this earth, this realm,
    this England,
This nurse, this teeming womb of royal
    kings,
Fear'd by their breed, and famous by
    their birth,
Renowned for their deeds as far from
    ⁀home,
(For Christian service, and true chivalry,)
As is the sepulchre in stubborn Jewry,
Of the world's ransom, blessed Mary's
    son :
This land of such dear souls, this dear
    dear land,
Dear for her reputation through the
    world,
Is now leas'd out (I die pronouncing
    it,)
Like to a tenement, or pelting farm :
England, bound in with the triumphant
    sea,
Whose rocky shore beats back the envi-
    ous siege
Of watery Neptune, is now bound in with
    shame,
With inky blots, and rotten parchment
    bonds ;
That England, that was wont to conquer
    others,
Hath made a shameful conquest of itself :

O, would the scandal vanish with my life,
How happy then were my ensuing death !
—*King Richard II., II., i.*

Shakespeare's heart evidently goes
with Henry V. in his invasion of
France and swells with patriotic
pride as he recounts the battle of
Agincourt.

Maritime adventure and discovery
were a great feature of the age.
About these Shakespeare is rather un-
accountably silent, though there are
abundant references to ships and sea-
faring life. The only apparent allusion is in *The Tempest*, where they
land on an undiscovered island.
Travellers' tales are more than once
subjects of satire, though Othello wins
the heart of Desdemona by his story
of wanderings which take him among

the Anthropophagi and the men whose
heads do grow beneath their shoulders.
A passage in *The Tempest* (III., iii.)
seems to suggest the idea that a race
of men gentler than the people of
Europe might be found in new coun-
tries. Potatoes, one of the pro-
ducts of discovery, are mentioned in
The Merry Wives of Windsor (V., v.)
and in *Troilus and Cressida* (V., ii).
It is evident, however, that Shakespeare's mind did not turn much in
that direction.

What was Shakespeare in religion ?
At the time when his intellectual
life began, a series of religious revolutions and counter - revolutions had
been closed by the Elizabethan settle-
ment; a compromise, framed by poli-
ticians for a political object, which

failed from the outset, as it has throughout, to satisfy religious aspiration, and has appeared to be successful only in periods of spiritual torpor. Puritanism, with its Genevan theology, was on the scene and was assailing the relics of Catholicism in the liturgy or the vestiary, and rebelling against the authority of the Bishops. Martin Marprelate was railing against mitres. More thoroughgoing than the Puritan, who was always for a national Establishment though purged of Popery, was the Brownist, who, like the Independent of an after day and the Baptist, was for an entire separation of Church from State. Brownism, as a revolutionary movement, was under the ban of the Government.

On the other hand, there were Roman
Catholics of two kinds; those of the
old school, national and patriotic,
ready to fight for England against
the Armada; and those of the new,
Ultramontane, and Jesuitical school,
who would have been ready to fight
with the Armada against England.
Conscientious Roman Catholics were
Recusants, refusing to attend the
worship prescribed by law and in-
curring fines by their non-attendance.
But besides these sects, religious con-
troversies and wars had not failed to
produce their natural effect in breed-
ing among men of more daring spirit,
or perhaps more libertine lives, total
scepticism or indifference to religion.
Among the Bohemians of the theatre
this tendency was likely to prevail.

Marlowe is maligned as a blatant atheist, an utterer of horrible and damnable opinions, who had written a book against the Trinity and defamed Christ. The imputation was extended to other Bohemians.

There seems, however, to have been freethinking of a more serious and respectable kind. In 1583 Giordano Bruno, in the course of the philosophical wanderings which ended in Rome and at the stake, visited England. He found much that was not to his liking; dirty streets, insolent domestics, and at Oxford Dons thinking more of their academic robes and their social position than of the advancement of learning, and with minds closed against new truths. But in London he found to his satisfaction comparative freedom of thought and speech. A circle, of which Sir Philip Sidney and Sir Fulke Greville were the chiefs and of which Bruno was a member, discussed questions of philosophy and science with closed doors. So far as social position was concerned, Shakespeare might possibly have found his way into that circle.

The State Church was in a very low condition. The bulk of the clergy had turned their coats under Mary and then again under Elizabeth. Of spiritual life there was probably little among them. They were greatly impoverished, and iconoclasm had dilapidated their churches. Their representatives in the Shakespearian drama are Sir Hugh Evans, who appears in *The Merry Wives of Windsor* as a boon companion and a butt, quarrelling like a dog and going out to fight a duel; and Sir Nathaniel, who plays a farcical part in *Love's Labour's Lost*.

There can be little difficulty in pronouncing Shakespeare a Conformist, as a servant of the Court was specially bound to be. At all events he was not a Nonconformist; for he ridicules the Nonconformists all round.

If men could be contented to be what they are, there were no fear in marriage : for young Charbon the Puritan, and old Poysam the Papist, howsoe'er their hearts are severed in religion, their heads are both one, they may joll horns together, like any deer i' the herd.

—*All's Well that Ends Well*, I., iii.

Though honesty be no Puritan, yet it will do no hurt; it will wear the surplice

68

of humility over the black gown of a big heart.

—*All's Well that Ends Well, I., iii.*

In *Twelfth-Night* (III., ii.) Sir Andrew Ague-cheek says " I had as lief be a Brownist as a politician."

There is perhaps a slight compliment to the conscientiousness of the Puritans in *Twelfth-Night,*—

Maria.—Marry, sir, sometimes he is a kind of Puritan.

Sir Andrew Ague-cheek.—O, if I thought that, I'd beat him like a dog.

Sir Toby Belch.—What, for being a Puritan ? thy exquisite reason, dear knight ?

Sir Andrew Ague-cheek.—I have no exquisite reason for't, but I have reason good enough.

Maria.—The devil a Puritan that he is, or any thing constantly but a time pleaser.

—*II., iii.*

Religious pretensions do not escape

ridicule. "Signior Bassanio," says
Gratiano in the *Merchant of Venice*,
" hear me :

If I do not put on a sober habit,
Talk with respect, and swear but now
   and then,
Wear prayer-books in my pocket, look
   demurely
Nay more, while grace is saying, hood
   mine eyes
Thus with my hat, and sigh, and say,
   amen ;
Use all the observance of civility,
Like one well studied in a sad ostent
To please his grandam, never trust me
   more.
          —II., ii.

Least of all can it be maintained
that Shakespeare was a Roman Catholic. Would it have been possible for
a Roman Catholic, even dramatically,
to have written this ?—

King Philip.—Here comes the holy legate
  of the pope.
Pandulph.—Hail, you anointed deputies
  of heaven !—

To thee king John, my holy errand is.
I Pandulph, of fair Milan cardinal,
And from pope Innocent the legate here,
Do, in his name, religiously demand,
Why thou against the church, our holy
    mother,
So wilfully dost spurn ; and, force per-
    force,
Keep Stephen Langton, chosen archbishop
Of Canterbury, from that holy see ?
This, in our 'foresaid holy father's name,
Pope Innocent, I do demand of thee.

    King John.—What earthly name to in-
    terrogatories,
Can task the free breath of a sacred
    king?
Thou canst not, cardinal, devise a name
So slight, unworthy, and ridiculous,
To charge me to an answer, as the pope.
Tell him this tale : and from the mouth of
    England,
Add thus much more,—That no Italian
    priest
Shall tithe or toil in our dominions ;
But as we under heaven are supreme head,
So, under him, that great supremacy,
Where we do reign, we will alone up-
    hold,
Without the assistance of a mortal hand :
So tell the pope ; all reverence set apart,
To him, and his usurp'd authority.

King Philip.—Brother of England, you
blaspheme in this.

King John.—Though you, and all the
kings of Christendom,
Are led so grossly by this meddling priest,
Dreading the curse that money may buy
out ;
And, by the merit of vile gold, dross,
dust,
Purchase corrupted pardon of a man,
Who, in that sale, sells pardon from him-
self ;
Though you, and all the rest, so grossly
led,
This juggling witchcraft with revenue
cherish ;
Yet I, alone, alone do me oppose
Against the pope, and count his friends
my foes.

—King John, III., i.

It is true Shakespeare treats Friars
respectfully in *Romeo and Juliet*, and
elsewhere. But this shows that he
was a large-minded artist, not that
he was a Roman Catholic. The Friars
were accessories of his Italian scenes.

To be sure he might think them,
though not ministers of a purer religion, characters more poetic, perhaps
more spiritual, than Sir Hugh Evans
and Sir Nathaniel. That his respect
for Friars was not religious seems to
be shown when he says,—

Clown.—As fit as ten groats is for the
hand of an attorney, as your French
crown for taffata punk, as Tib's rush
for Tom's fore-finger, as a pancake for
Shrove-Tuesday, a morris for May-day,
as the nail to his hole, the cuckold to
his horn, as a scolding quean to a
wrangling knave, as the nun's lip to
the friar's mouth ; nay, as the pud-
ding to his skin.

—All's Well that Ends Well, II., ii.

The ghost and the purgatory in
Hamlet are evidently a mere part
of the fiction. No belief is indicated
in purgatory any more than in ghosts.

A Conformist we may safely take Shakespeare to have been ; whether he was a church-goer, we have no means of telling. Atheistical or irreligious, he evidently was not. His general spirit is religious. With him, to be where " holy bells knoll to church," is synonymous with civilized life. The Almighty has fixed his canon against self-slaughter. In *Twelfth - Night* Malvolio, here evidently serious, when asked whether he assents to a degrading opinion of the soul, answers that he thinks nobly of the soul, and by no means assents to the opinion. In *Measure for Measure* there is a respectful allusion to the doctrine of the Redemption.

Isabella.—   Alas ! Alas !
Why, all the souls that were, were forfeit
    once ;

74

And He that might the vantage best have
   took,
Found out the remedy.

                     —II., ii.

In *The Merchant of Venice,* mercy
in man reflects an attribute of God.

On the other hand, when Shakespeare touches the problem of human
existence or that of the world to
come, we cannot help feeling that
we are in contact with a mind
more like that of Giordano Bruno,
or rather that of the Elizabethan
liberals, than that of an orthodox
Anglican Divine. The soliloquy in
Hamlet presents nothing sceptical ;
yet it and Hamlet's general utter-
ances are pervaded by the spirit of
one to whom the state of man, present
and future, is an unsolved mystery.
We do not know "in that sleep of

death what dreams may come." The world beyond the grave is "the un-discovered country from whose bourn no traveller returns." To die is to "go we know not where." "We are such stuff as dreams are made on ; and our little life is rounded with a sleep." This globe of ours "like an unsubstantial pageant, will vanish and leave not a ~~wreck~~ *rack* behind." That Shakespeare himself speaks in such passages cannot be affirmed, but may surely, without much improbability, be divined.

Among the absurdities of the Bacon-ian theory, not one is greater than the idea that Bacon could have passed, in changing his kind of composition, from the scientific orthodoxy of his acknow-ledged works to the frame of mind characteristic of the Shakespearian drama.

Of the greatness of Shakespeare's genius, this is not, any more than of the features of his art, the place to speak. ⌈His genius is so great that it has raised the whole Elizabethan drama to a height of reputation which probably none of its other writers, with the possible exception of Marlowe, could of themselves have attained. ⌈